BOOK CLUB IN A BOX

Bookclub-in-a-Box presents the discussion companion for Jhumpa Lahiri's novel

The Namesake

Published by Mariner Books, 2004, Houghton Mifflin Company.
ISBN: 0-618-48522-8

Quotations used in this guide have been taken from the text of the paperback edition of **The Namesake**. All information taken from other sources is acknowledged.

This discussion companion for **The Namesake** has been prepared and written by Marilyn Herbert, originator of Bookclub-in-a-Box. Marilyn Herbert. B.Ed., is a teacher, librarian, speaker and writer. Bookclub-in-a-Box is a unique guide to current fiction and classic literature intended for book club discussions, educational study seminars, and personal pleasure. For more information about the Bookclub-in-a-Box team, visit our website.

Bookclub-in-a-Box discussion companion for The Namesake

ISBN 10: 1-897082-39-8
ISBN 13: 978-1897082393

This guide reflects the perspective of the Bookclub-in-a-Box team and is the sole property of Bookclub-in-a-Box.

CONTACT INFORMATION: SEE BACK COVER.

BOOKCLUB-IN-A-BOX

Jhumpa Lahiri's The Namesake

BOOKCLUB-IN-A-BOX

Readers and Leaders Guide

Each Bookclub-in-a-Box guide is clearly and effectively organized to give you information and ideas for a lively discussion, as well as to present the major highlights of the novel. The format, with a Table of Contents, allows you to pick and choose the specific points you wish to talk about. It does not have to be used in any prescribed order. In fact, it is meant to support, not determine, your discussion.

You Choose What to Use.

You may find that some information is repeated in more than one section and may be cross-referenced so as to provide insight on the same idea from different angles.

The guide is formatted to give you extra space to make your own notes.

How to Begin

Relax and look forward to enjoying your bookclub.

With Bookclub-in-a-Box as your behind the scenes support, there is little for you to do in the way of preparation.

Some readers like to review the guide after reading the novel; some before. Either way, the guide is all you will need as a companion for your discussion. You may find that the guide's interpretation, information, and background have sparked other ideas not included.

Having read the novel and armed with Bookclub-in-a-Box, you will be well prepared to lead or guide or listen to the discussion at hand.

Lastly, if you need some more 'hands-on' support, feel free to contact us. (See Contact Information)

What to Look For

Each Bookclub-in-a-Box guide is divided into easy-to-use sections, which include points on characters, themes, writing style and structure, literary or historical background, author information, and other pertinent features unique to the novel being discussed. These may vary slightly from guide to guide.

INTERPRETATION OF EACH NOVEL REFLECTS THE PERSPECTIVE OF THE BOOKCLUB-IN-A-BOX TEAM.

Do We Need to Agree?

THE ANSWER TO THIS QUESTION IS NO.

If we have sparked a discussion or a debate on certain points, then we are happy. We invite you to share your group's alternative findings and experiences with us. You can respond on-line at our website or contact us through our Contact Information. We would love to hear from you.

Discussion Starters

There are as many ways to begin a bookclub discussion as there are members in your group. If you are an experienced group, you will already have your favorite ways to begin. If you are a newly formed group or a group looking for new ideas, here are some suggestions.

Ask for people's impressions of the novel. (This will give you some idea about which parts of the unit to focus on.)

- Identify a favorite or major character.

- Identify a favorite or major idea.

- Begin with a powerful or pertinent quote. (not necessarily from the novel)

- Discuss the historical information of the novel. (not applicable to all novels)

- If this author is familiar to the group, discuss the range of his/her work and where this novel stands in that range.

- Use the discussion topics and questions in the Bookclub-in-a-Box guide.

If you have further suggestions for discussion starters, be sure to share them with us and we will share them with others.

Above All, Enjoy Yourselves

INTRODUCTION

Novel Quickline

The Namesake is a novel about the start of a new life, a new culture, a new country. The parents of our story, Ashoke and Ashima, have moved from India to America. Ashoke is to be a doctoral candidate in electrical engineering at MIT (The Massachusetts Institute of Technology), located in Cambridge, Massachusetts. With him is his new bride, Ashima. The novel opens with the birth of their first child, a son.

Immediately there is a clash of cultures – the baby must be named, an important step in every baby's acculturation. In the Bengali tradition, this is a relaxed and honored practice. The child is usually given two names: a pet or nickname to be used within the family, and a good name to be used outside the family circle. According to Bengali tradition, the Hindu ceremony for naming a baby takes place at home and lasts anywhere from eleven to forty-one days after birth – but that is in India.

The Gangulis are now in America, where everything moves more quickly. They are told that they cannot take the baby home until a name is registered on his birth certificate. What are they to do? The honor of naming this child belongs to Ashima's grandmother, who lives in India. The letter that will declare the baby's good name has not arrived and the parents have not even begun to think of a pet name. Suddenly there is pressure.

The name of the Russian writer Gogol comes to mind. Ashoke had been caught in a life-threatening train accident when he was younger and had been miraculously saved when someone noticed the movement of his hand in which he grasped a page from a book of short stories by Nikolai Gogol.

He tries the name out on the baby.

> *"Hello, Gogol," [his father whispers] ... "Gogol," he repeats, satisfied. The baby turns his head with an expression of extreme consternation and yawns."* (p.28)

Despite the baby's worried reaction, both parents approve of the name, because it represents the birth of the son and the re-birth of the father. *"Besides, it's only a pet name, not to be taken seriously, simply something to put on the certificate for now to release them from the hospital."* (p.29)

What cultural ideas do we inherit from our parents? In an immigrant situation, if these cultural ideas and perspectives clash with the new environment, how is that clash managed? Do people grow into their names, or do their names shape them?

Keys to the Novel

Normally, the keys to a novel highlight the special themes and focus points the author wants to emphasize. In the case of **The Namesake**, the features of style are what make Lahiri's book special. The main thematic elements will be discussed more fully on page 27.

Short Story Framework

- The primary characteristic of the short story is its emphasis on a single literary feature: a plot event, a short period of time, a single character, the setting, or the mood of the story. Lahiri's training and experience has been as a writer of short stories, and we see in **The Namesake** that she applies her short story talents to this full-length novel by using the idea of the name as the single defining feature of who Gogol is and who he becomes. (see Author Information, p.8)

Names

- Lahiri's book encourages us to look at names in a totally new way. Our name is our overcoat. It presents us to the outside world and is the first clear layer of identity. (see Name, p.53)

Narrative Technique

- Lahiri tells her story using visual markers and cues, as if she is using a verbal camera. Although all novels use symbols and images to create pictures in our imagination, Lahiri gives us instant snapshots in place of longer descriptions and ongoing dialogue.

- The scenes are short, and there are spaces between events. There is a distinct feeling that the reader is viewing the characters through a filtered screen. As the novel moves forward, the sentences and paragraphs enlarge the characters and advance the plot. At the same time, Lahiri unwraps her layers of meaning and interpretation and brings them into sharp focus.

- For this reason, it is easy to see how the novel has been successfully recreated as a film by director Mira Nair. (see The Film, p.67)
  Consider the film in connection to the novel.

Author Information

- Jhumpa Lahiri was born in 1967, in London, England, to immigrant parents from Kolkata, India. (Kolkata was formerly known as Calcutta. It changed its name in January 2001.) When she was young, the family moved to the United States, and Lahiri was raised in Rhode Island. Her father was a university librarian and her mother a school teacher. (see Symbols, Overcoat, p.54)

- Lahiri has three master's degrees and one PhD, all in English and creative-writing studies. She trained and worked as a teacher up until her extraordinary success as a writer. In 2000, she became one of the youngest winners of the Pulitzer Prize for Fiction for her very first publishing effort, a book of short stories called **The Interpreter of Maladies**. Since then she has married, had a son, and has written this novel, **The Namesake**.

- The novel is autobiographical in the sense that Lahiri is exploring familiar territory. She is about the same age as Gogol, whose parents, like hers, are from West Bengal. As a result, she is well acquainted with the expat Bengali community and with the struggle of first-generation American-born children over the issue of cultural identity and belonging.

- Lahiri comes from three cultures – British, American, and Indian. Because her name is Indian, people assume that her identity and nationality are the same. So when they ask where she comes from, her answer – Rhode Island – is not readily accepted.

- Lahiri overlaps with her characters. Like Moushumi, she feels closest to being British, since Britain is the country of her birth. Like Gogol (and Moushumi), Lahiri grew up as the child of immigrants who are far from their origins. There is a strong sense of separation between the experiences, values, and education of the parents and those of the children, and it is this separation that leads straight into Lahiri's theme of identity. (see Identity, p.53)

What defines your identity more closely – birthplace, childhood home, or cultural heritage?

- Lahiri grew up with the tradition of good names and pet names. Jhumpa, which is her pet name, came to be used publicly because her school decided that it was the easier of her two names to pronounce. This, of course, is also Gogol's experience.

- Lahiri is married to Alberto Vourvoulias Bush, a man of Greek descent who was born in Guatemala and raised in Mexico. Together with their young son, Octavio, they live in Brooklyn, New York. The novel is dedicated to Lahiri's husband and son, whom she says she calls by other names.

- The Namesake was released as a film in 2007, and Lahiri has a cameo role in it as Aunt Jhumpa. It is directed by Mira Nair (*Monsoon Wedding*). (see The Film, p.67)

Demographic Information

- West Bengal is located on the eastern fringe of India, bounded by Bangladesh to the east and the Bay of Bengal to the south. In historic times, the area included what is now Bangladesh. From the thirteenth to the fifteenth centuries, Bengal was under Islamic rule, and in the fifteenth century, the Europeans, including the British, arrived. By the eighteenth century, the British East India Company controlled all of India, including the area of Bengal.

- Independence came in 1947, followed by partition. Bengal was divided into West Bengal, with a Hindu majority, and East Bengal, with mostly Muslims. East Bengal became Bangladesh in 1971. Between the time of partition and the establishment of Bangladesh, approximately sixteen million people moved to greater India, including the West Bengal zone.

- West Bengal has been home to India's Nobel Laureate in Literature, Rabindranath Tagore and Amartya Sen, winner of the Nobel Prize in Economics, as well as famous film director Satyajit Ray, singer Kishore Kumar, and musician Ravi Shankar.

- According to a 2000 census, the fastest-growing group of South Asian immigrants to the U.S. are the Indians, who now number about 1.7 million. This group includes people from India, Bangladesh, Pakistan, Nepal, and Sri Lanka, 75 percent of whom have post-secondary education.

CHARACTERIZATION

CHARACTERIZATION

General Comments

E. M. Forster, in **Aspects of the Novel**, describes two types of fictional characters – round or flat. Rounder characters need a writer's and a reader's interpretation. By definition, there is more to them, and we see change and development. (The Russian masters tended to round out their characters.) Flat characters rarely change; they simply reflect the shape and makeup of the round characters. Lahiri has created a strong division between these two distinct sets of characters. The first set includes those characters whose thoughts we are allowed to enter – Gogol, Ashoke, Ashima, and later, Moushumi. These are complex characters, who are busy exploring and defining their identities. Some of the characters do it more quickly; some do it better. Lahiri concentrates on and develops this group because she has sympathy for the task they are facing.

The others, Ruth, Maxine, and Sonia, are reflected only through the eyes and minds of the main characters. We never know what they are thinking; we only see their reactions to the main characters.

This brings us to the author, Nikolai Gogol, who is important to the understanding of the Gogol of our story.

Nikolai Gogol and The Overcoat

- Nikolai Gogol is considered Russia's best but perhaps least comprehensible writer. In his short life, 1809 to 1852, he produced many works that were dramatic and satiric in nature. Unlike other Russian writers, Gogol turned his focus to the flaws of the human character, not to the characters themselves. He flattened them and placed them into absurd situations. Lahiri's novel is based on Gogol's famous short story "The Overcoat."

- Gogol was a genius, but he was also a strangely disturbed personality. He drove away both friends and colleagues with his hypochondria, his melancholy, and his depression. The cause of his death is widely thought to be self-starvation.

- Gogol's story is about the misfortunes of a government clerk who is mistreated and ignored by his fellow workers, primarily because he has no personality and no name of his own. He was supposed to have been named after a saint, but an appropriate one could not be found in time, so he was baptized as Akaky Akakievich, which simply means "son of Akaky."

- During the course of the story, Akaky buys an overcoat that he hopes will get him noticed; it is stolen, and when he tries to get it back, he is stalled at every turn. Then he gets sick and dies. That is the first part of the story. In the second part, he comes back to haunt his fellow workers.

- Because Akaky has no clear identity of his own, his name becomes an ill-fitting cover, just like his overcoat, which never suited him or his station properly. It seems that the overcoat's only function was to cause people to make fun of him.

- The Gogol of Lahiri's novel got his oddly fitting name in an incident of similar bureaucratic red tape when his parents needed a name in a hurry. This name was never meant to be permanent, but it ended up becoming the overcoat that our Gogol does not wear comfortably. Our Gogol also has no personal identity. Instead he is named for an absurdly strange Russian author, a fact that has nothing to do with him, either as an American or as a Bengali.

- Consider this last similarity between the two stories: just as the clerk dies partway through the Russian short story, Gogol's father dies midway through the book. Although the relationship between father and son is not the same as that of the clerk and his fellow workers, Gogol's father becomes a strong and haunting presence for his son. He has a greater effect on Gogol in death than he had in life.

Gogol

- When Gogol is born his mother feels sad for him. *"She has never known of a person entering the world so alone, so deprived."* (p.25) She knows that in India, this child and mother would have been surrounded by family and friends, and the child would have been born in the comfort and security of home, not hospital. But, as soon as the novel begins, the reader can see immediately that Gogol is to be unconnected to many things around him.

- As a child, Gogol was comfortable with his name. It all *"seem[ed] perfectly normal."* (p.66) He never knew anything different, and the only thing that made him sad is that he couldn't find "Gogol" on a key chain like other American names. But as he grows into the wider world and travels between America and India, he begins to realize that his name (but only his last name) identifies him there. In India, the name Ganguli is perfectly normal and very common. His struggle continues. (see Alliteration, p.43)

- The turning point for Gogol comes one Halloween, when his last name is transformed by pranksters into "Gang-green." Gogol is suddenly aware that his parents speak with pronounced accents and that merchants therefore speak to him as if he were the translator for his parents. He becomes acutely aware that his name is very, very odd.

- He feels betrayed by his parents, especially when he learns at school that his namesake, the Russian Gogol, was a severely depressed personality. Couldn't he have been a depressed romantic, someone to look up to? *"I don't get it. How could you name me after someone so strange? No one takes me seriously."* (p.100) How then can he take himself seriously?

- Gogol is a typical American teenager who hates his name, *"hates having constantly to explain ... hates having to tell people that it doesn't mean anything "in Indian" ... hates having to live with it, with a pet name turned good name, day after day, second after second."* (p.76)

- It takes Gogol a long time to consider changing his pet name to a more formal one, but eventually he legally turns the Russian Nikolai into Nikhil. But even this action leaves him conflicted, because he is not fully comfortable as either Nikhil or Gogol. He realizes that not only is he *not* unique, he is indefinable, even to himself.

- Ironically, Gogol becomes an architect, which means he is trained to pay attention to detail. However, he neglects so very many meaningful details about his parents, his culture, and Moushumi.

Ashima, Ashoke

- Ashima and Ashoke adhere closely to the customs with which they were raised, never questioning their cultural heritage nor their identity. Accordingly, they agree to an arranged marriage. Just before they meet for the first time, Ashima finds Ashoke's shoes in the hallway. *"Unable to resist a sudden and overwhelming urge, [she] stepped into the shoes at her feet. Lingering sweat from the owner's feet mingled with hers, causing her heart to race."* (p.8) She doesn't learn his name until after they are engaged, and even then, Ashima abides by Bengali tradition, and never calls her husband by his good name. They enter the strange new land of America together but still as strangers to each other. But by the end of the story, we see that their relationship has deepened and is set on the kind of enduring base that eludes Gogol in all his relationships.

   > *Eight thousand miles away in Cambridge, she has come to know him ... At night, lying beside her in bed, he listens to her describe the events of her day.* (p.10)

- Both Ashoke and Ashima are involved in literary pursuits. Ashoke comes to Boston as a PhD student in engineering who reads classic Russian literature with a love passed down to him by his grandfather. He enjoys visiting the university's library stacks, where he finds shelves of Russian novels, including those by Gogol. Ashima works part-time in a library, surrounded by words and ideas. The creative skills of her artist father are also passed down a generation later to her son, Gogol, who eventually becomes an architect.

- The lonely young couple look for and assemble other ex-pat Bengali families, and they spend Sundays in each other's homes like family. Continuity of culture and commonality play a large part in the friendships that Ashima and Ashoke form with others. Slowly, they adjust to having a foot on each of two continents. Ashima's name means "without borders," and after the children are grown, she decides to live half time in the United States and half time in India.

- As a young student, Ashoke survived a serious train wreck, saved by a page from Nikolai Gogol's book. On his son's fourteenth birthday, Ashoke tries to give Gogol a copy of this book and to tell him the story of his name, but Gogol, a typical teenager, is not interested in his father's tale.

> *Gogol leans over toward the stereo to turn the volume down a bit. He would have preferred The Hitchhiker's Guide to the Galaxy or even another copy of The Hobbit to replace the one he lost last summer in Calcutta ... He has never been inspired to read a word of Gogol, or any Russian writer. ... He has never been told why he was really named Gogol, doesn't know about the accident that had nearly killed his father. He thinks his father's limp is the consequence of an injury playing soccer in his teens. He's been told only half the truth about Gogol: that his father is a fan.* (p.75)

Maxine

- Maxine Ratliffe is an all-American girl with seemingly no identity issues, despite the fact that she lives with her parents. This may be part of Gogol's attraction to her. Maxine is an assistant editor of art books and is independent and free by nature, qualities that intrigue Gogol, who rarely feels independent.

- The Ratliffe home is a warm, open, and inviting place, filled with physical clutter. It appears to Gogol that Maxine's life is set in stark contrast to his own family life, and yet there is a similar intergenerational bond that Gogol's parents would likely have experienced with their extended family in India. In addition, there is the same collection of friends on hand that he had growing up. Gogol doesn't see the connections; he sees only a dividing line, and he prefers to stand on the side that brings him closer to an American identity and further from an Indian one. Gogol is still trying on distinctly different coats of individuality.

    [At the Ratliffe cottage, Gogol] grows to appreciate being utterly disconnected from the world ... The family seems to possess every piece of the landscape ... every tree and blade of grass ... It is a place that has been good to them, as much a part of them as a member of the family. The idea of returning year after year to a single place appeals to Gogol deeply. (p.154, 155)

- Gogol had many trips with his family, traveling through Canada and the United States, or returning to India. Yet, *"he feels no nostalgia for the vacations he's spent with his family, and he realizes now that they were never really true vacations at all. Instead they were overwhelming, disorienting expeditions ... sightseeing in places they did not belong to and intended never to see again."* (p.155) Gogol falls in love equally with Maxine and with his perception of her family. But he is always aware that *"his immersion in Maxine's family is a betrayal of his own."* (p.141)

- Against his better judgment, Gogol takes Maxine to his home for a visit. Gogol outlines what Maxine should expect and lists a number of restrictions and conditions of behavior. *"[Maxine] sees them as a single afternoon's challenge, an anomaly never to be repeated."* (p.146)

- Their drop-in lunch is awkward: Maxine brings a number of inappropriate gifts; Ashima tries hard to please, has dressed especially for company and has prepared a feast, which Gogol knows has taken his mother an inordinate amount of time to prepare. But Maxine is relaxed and friendly and by the time they leave, there are *"hugs and kisses good-bye, initiated by Maxine, his parents reciprocating clumsily."* (p.150) Gogol is relieved to leave them, not realizing that he will never see his father again.

- For all her open-hearted worldliness, Maxine does not understand Gogol or where he comes from. Maxine knows Gogol as Nikhil and thinks that his nickname Gogol is simply a cute story, which she promptly forgets about. For Gogol, there is a sense of harshness to *"this essential fact about his life slipping from her mind."* (p.156)

- During the mourning period for Ashoke, Maxine comes to see Gogol. Not knowing about Indian mourning customs nor understanding Gogol's conflicted emotions, she talks to him in the context of her own customs and values. She tells him he can't stay with his mother forever, that he must come back and resume his life with her. But Gogol has already crossed back over the border between his separate lives.

  > *"I'm so sorry," he hears her say to his mother, aware that his father's death does not affect Maxine in the least. "You guys can't stay with your mother forever ... You know that." She says it gently, puts her hand to his cheek. He stares at her, takes her hand and puts it back in her lap ...*
  >
  > *"It might do you good ... to get away from all this."*
  >
  > *"I don't want to get away."* (p.182)

Moushumi

- Gogol first meets Moushumi at his fourteenth birthday party, the occasion of which is another reason for his parents to invite their Bengali friends. One of the forty or so guests is thirteen-year-old Moushumi, who recently emigrated to the United States from England.

> ... *Gogol and Moushumi have nothing to say to each other. Moushumi sits cross-legged on the floor, in glasses with maroon plastic frames and a puffy polka-dotted headband holding back her thick, chin-length hair ... She is reading a well-thumbed paperback copy of* **Pride and Prejudice** *while the other children, Gogol included, watch* **The Love Boat** *and* **Fantasy Island** *... Occasionally one of the children asks Moushumi to say something, anything, in her English accent ... "I detest American television," Moushumi eventually declares.*
> (p.73)

- By the time Gogol meets her again, an arrangement orchestrated by both of their mothers, they are equally struck by the many things they have in common. He likes the fact that Moushumi once knew him as Gogol. This fact allows him to instantly relax.

> *He had not expected to enjoy himself, to be attracted to her in the least. It strikes him that there is no term for what they once were to each other. Their parents were friends, not they. ... Until they'd met tonight, he had never seen her outside the context of her family, or she his. He decides that it is her very familiarity that makes him curious about her.* (p.199)

- Both Gogol and Moushumi had spent years with other people trying to avoid, ignore, and remove the Indian part of their heritage from their lives. But for both, none of these relationships succeeded. For that reason, perhaps, it felt so easy for the two of them to come together. Instead of fighting the part of their identity they were born with, they sank into it with a sense of relief.

> *Gogol and Moushumi agree that it's better to give into these expectations than to put up a fight. It's what they deserve, they joke, for having listened to their mothers, and for getting together in the first place, and the fact that they are united in their resignation makes the consequences somewhat bearable.* (p.219)

- But Moushumi, even more than Gogol, is searching to reinvent herself in any number of ways. She is more dislocated than Gogol, because she is two steps removed from India. She came from England to the United States at the very awkward age of thirteen. In addition, she lived for a while in France, where she met her first fiancé, Graham, and her lover (much later) Dimitri. Like Gogol's relationship with Maxine, Moushumi and Graham were on opposite sides of the ocean of cultural identity. Her parents tried to accept him and his fractured American family (p.216), and Graham found her family *"taxing ... the culture repressed ... and provincial."* (p.217) Eventually they split up.

- Moushumi is independent in a different way than Maxine. Where Maxine is a separate but integral part of her family unit, Moushumi finds it difficult to be fully immersed in her family and culture. *"Sometimes she would sit at a restaurant alone, at the bar, ordering sushi or a sandwich and a glass of wine, simply to remind herself that she was still capable of being on her own ... at her wedding, she'd privately vowed that she'd never grow fully dependent on her husband, as her mother has."* (p.247)

- She begins to find marriage to Gogol confining and, unknown to him, plans to accept a research fellowship in France. She reconnects with Dimitri and launches into an affair with him, an *"affair [that] causes her to feel strangely at peace, the complication of it calming her, structuring her day."* (p.267) When Gogol finally learns about their liaison, he first feels humiliated and deceived, but then *"he was strangely calm – in the moment that his marriage was effectively severed he was on solid ground with her for the first time in months."* (p.282)

Sonia

- As is often the case with second-born immigrant children, Sonia (Gogol's sister) has an easier time fitting into her societal cloak than does her brother. For starters, her parents had learned their lesson about naming children – Sonia is given only one name.

- Everything is easier for Sonia, especially dating. Nothing is said when she brings home her future non-Indian, half-Jewish, half-Chinese husband, Ben.

Ruth

- Ruth is Gogol's first girlfriend, his first foray out of his Indian world. Significantly, he meets her on the train and recognizes her from campus. (see Train, p.60) They talk a lot about his trips to India, and he is happy that she is interested. It occurs to him *"that he has never spoken of his experiences in India to any American friend."* (p.112) He certainly does not speak of them later with Maxine.

- But Gogol and Ruth are still young, and each lives at home. Like her biblical namesake, this Ruth is compliant, and she understands about not being able to visit Gogol in his home. *"Much as he longs to see her, he cannot picture her at the kitchen table on Pemberton Road, in her jeans and her bulky sweater, politely eating his mother's food.*

He cannot imagine being with her in the house where he is still Gogol." (p.115) This changes with Maxine, but only slightly.

- By the time Gogol takes a train trip home in his senior year, he and Ruth are no longer together. *"They'd begun fighting, both admitting in the end that something had changed."* (p.120)

Graham

- Graham is a former boyfriend and fiancé of Moushumi's. His name is from Old English and means a "gravel area." In a clash of their cultures, he certainly rubs her the wrong way. (see Moushumi, p.21)

Dimitri

- Moushumi's new lover is Dimitri, a man whose name has both a French and a Russian connection. It originates from the Greek, *Demetrius*, meaning the follower of the goddess, Demeter. In a sense, Moushumi is a goddess, but she has followed Dimitri and tracked him down.

FOCUS POINTS AND THEMES

Names (Identity)

Naming Custom

Alienation, Loss

Assimilation

FOCUS POINTS AND THEMES

Lahiri uses her characters and the idea of their names to explore many of the novel's concerns relating to identity (both personal and cultural), alienation, assimilation (connection and betrayal), and others. She looks at these topics in two dimensions – vertically through the parents and the children, and laterally through the couples, Ashoke and Ashima, as well as Gogol and his two partners, Maxine and Moushumi.

Names (Identity)

- Our name is our overcoat. It presents us to the outside world and is the first clear indicator of our identity. Our name differs from the protective layer of our real skin, because our name's influence seeps underneath and lodges itself in our psychological consciousness. This general consciousness is then re-projected outwardly as our identity. (see Narration, p.42)

- A name is the first step in the process of introducing ourselves to others and can sometimes precede us, for example, in a letter, a resumé, or even a phone call. Some people are instantly recognized by a single name – for instance, Jesus, Madonna, Shakespeare, or Prince.

- Our name is just one of many specific characteristics that define who we are, yet we don't tend to give our own name a lot of thought or weight. Parents are the ones who agonize over choosing the correct name for their offspring. The recipients of those names rarely challenge or change the choice. Lahiri tells her readers not to take a name lightly.

  Have you changed your name in any way, or do you know anyone who has? What was the reason for the change?

- A name can also serve to protect or separate us from the outer world. It keeps us from being anonymous. Affectionate nicknames are usually given by those closest to us in the inner worlds of friends and family. Conversely, a name can create a target or be a weapon for bully behavior.

- Names change with popularity and use, and their significance alters with time. Gogol goes on a school trip to a cemetery, where he learns that names can die just as people do. Gogol is comforted by the fact that other immigrants to America were also the *"bearers of unthinkable, obsolete names."* (p.70)

- America is not the only place where names are changed. When the British came to India, they anglicized many names. For example, Ganguli was shortened from the original Gangopadhyay. (p.67) **In the past, many immigrants to America have westernized their names. Consider the positive and negative effects of this practice.**

- Gogol knows that his name will have no permanent marker (a gravestone). According to Hindu custom, his death, like his father's, will be marked with cremation. But for the time being, his name perpetuates the existence of a famous and long dead Russian author.

- Gogol discovers that many people have changed their names, especially immigrants to Ellis Island. (p.97) Lahiri tells us that Nikolai Gogol also renamed himself from Gogol-Yanovsky to Gogol.

- When he enters his freshman year at university, Gogol does the same. As his father tells him, *"in America anything is possible"* (p.100), and Gogol reinvents himself as Nikhil Ganguli. But the transition is not easy.

  > *There is only one complication: he doesn't feel like Nikhil. Not yet. Part of the problem is that the people who now know him as Nikhil have no idea that he used to be Gogol ... After eighteen years of Gogol, two months of Nikhil feel scant, inconsequential ... At times he still feels his old name, painfully and without warning, the way his front tooth had unbearably throbbed in recent weeks after a filling.* (p.105)

- Our name is the overcoat of our identity, one that we can put on or take off at will. It can make us visible, it can encourage anonymity, or it can render us invisible, like Gogol's Akaky. Perhaps this is one possible meaning of Dostoyevsky's statement, that we all come out of Gogol's overcoat. (see Dostoyevsky, p.45)

- Our names tell the short (or long) story of who we are. Consequently, Lahiri zooms in on the names of some of her other characters.

Sonia

- Gogol's sister, Sonia, is not given two names but is named Sonali, out of which comes the nickname, Sonia. Her identity overcoat has a Russian link that connects her to her brother, it is a common European and South American name, and it is also the name of the Italian wife of one of India's prime ministers (Rajiv Gandhi). With such a versatile name, Sonia can never be classified simply as an immigrant's child; she is a citizen of the world.

- In typical sisterly fashion, Sonia renames Gogol as "Goggles."

Moushumi

- Moushumi always felt that her name was a curse, because no one could pronounce it properly, and so it was often shortened to "Moose." She disliked *"being the only Moushumi [she] knew."* (p.239) And yet she is comforted by the nickname "Mouse" that her lover, Dimitri, gives to her. From Mouse to Moose is the distance of a single letter, yet it represents an ocean of emotional divide. (see Ocean, p.59)

- Of all the characters in the novel, Moushumi should have been in complete emotional sync with Gogol, but she is the one who insensitively discloses that he was once known as Gogol. This happens when they are with Moushumi's friends, Astrid and Donald. Because they are not Gogol's friends, he feels betrayed. *"It has been years since he's been Gogol to anyone other than his family, their friends. It sounds as it always does, simple, impossible, absurd."* (p.243) This trivial incident threatens to become a trite party anecdote, which will forever identify him as strange and insignificant. Gogol still has issues.

Naming Custom

- Each culture has specific customs that surround the naming of a baby. The one that pertains to this novel is the Hindu ceremony, *namakarana*, which takes place eleven to forty-one days after the baby is born, either in the home or the temple. The new name is whispered into the baby's ear by the father. Ashoke does that in a makeshift ceremony at the hospital. (see Novel Quickline, p.5)

- According to Bengali custom, the parents take their time and choose two of the best possible names for their child: a good name *"to represent dignified and enlightened qualities,"* and a pet name, which will be *"a persistent remnant of childhood, a reminder that life is not always so serious, so formal, so complicated. They are a reminder, too, that one is not all things to all people."* (p.26)

Compare this to the naming ceremonies with which you are familiar.

Alienation and Loss   *geography, name, culture*

Geography

- Immigrants suffer from the physical separation from everything and everyone they know and love. Even when they move to a place that has a large ex-patriot community of their own nationality, there is an impact.

- When they first move from India, Ashima and Ashoke suffer from loneliness, being so far from their families and all that is familiar to them. *"In some senses Ashoke and Ashima live the lives of the extremely aged, those for whom everyone they once knew and loved is lost, those who survive and are consoled by memory alone."* (p.63)

- In a second move, they change from a house in the city to one in the suburbs. Ashima finds this move more difficult than the original move across the ocean. For Ashima, *"being a foreigner ... is a sort of lifelong pregnancy – a perpetual wait, a constant burden, a continuous feeling out of sorts ... The previous life has vanished, replaced by something more complicated and demanding."* (p.49, 50)

- Ashima loses not only her country but a loved one from each generation – her father, her grandmother, and her husband. If life is seen as a journey, then each relationship is a different phase of that journey. (see Journey, p.57) Each loss that disrupts the natural order of her life brings about another degree of alienation and further removes her emotional base of support.

- It is interesting to note that when her father and grandmother die, the whole family returns to India. When Ashoke dies in Cleveland, Gogol makes the trip alone. Ashima has reached her limit; Gogol must face his, head-on.

- But as much as Ashima once felt isolated from her Indian home, she feels a profound sense of loss as she prepares to return to India. Now a widow, Ashima *"feels overwhelmed by the thought of the move she is about to make, to the city that was once home and is now in its own way foreign."* (p.278) She will miss her library friends, Gogol, Sonia, and especially the memories of Ashoke in their American home. It was here that she fell in love with him.

Name

- It is not only a physical move that can trigger alienation and loss. Lahiri's treatment of "name" shows that it can have the same effect. Gogol initially accepts his name because that is all he knows. As he grows up, his name isolates him, yet he suffers a further distinct sense of loss when he discovers that he is not unique but is named for another Gogol. (p.90)

- There is loss once again when both Maxine and Moushumi throw Gogol back into the old domain of his pet name. Each woman trivializes the name that had identified him for so many years. His grasp of his personal identity is rocked to and fro with each dissociation.

Cultural Divide

- Gogol's sense of alienation is reflected even further in the community's self-doubt. Lahiri introduces us to the term ABCD – American-born confused *deshi*. *Desh* means home country; therefore, *deshi* (also written as *desi*) refers to countrymen. In the diaspora, many South Asians call themselves *deshi*.

- Gogol does not consider himself to be an ABCD, because he never thinks of India as his home country. (p.118) He spends a lot of time and energy avoiding other ABCD's, whose only connection is a tenuous link to Calcutta. This is certainly true of the makeshift "family" that Gogol's parents assembled. Many immigrants gravitate to the common denominators of geography, language, and culture.

- One of the things Gogol contends with is the perception by others as to where he belongs. At the Ratliffe cottage, a guest is convinced that Gogol was born and raised in India on the basis of his name alone. (p.157) (This is an experience Lahiri shares.) Children from foreign cultures who have visibly different appearances and names are always assumed to be from "away." As a result, they may sense they are from two places instead of one and may feel divided and separated not only from the previous generation, but also from their peers. In reality, they are people who are strangers to their fellow compatriots as much as they are to the wider "other" community.

  This is a very common experience, and many people zero in on the smallest of connections with each other in order to play the "geography/name" game. How does this add to or detract from their relationships with others?

- Gogol feels the keenest sense of alienation and loss when he celebrates his twenty-first birthday with Maxine and her family. With them, Gogol feels free, but free of what? The entire experience has a double edge. As *"everybody sings 'Happy Birthday,' this group who has known him for only one evening [and who] will forget him the next day,"* (p.158) Gogol suddenly thinks of his father. Ashoke is alone in Cleveland in a barren apartment, and Ashima, his mother, is alone in their Pemberton Road home. The significance of this only comes to Gogol much later.

- We learn that while Ashoke is dying far away from her (as did her parents and other relatives), Ashima is addressing the family Christmas cards using Ashoke's real name and Gogol's pet name. She is the keeper of the names. In a single sentence, Ashima sums up the family's life in this country, and we are again immediately aware of the differences between her life in the States and what it would have been had she stayed in India. Before she left India, she lived in her parents' home and for a very brief while in her husband's family's home, a place where she would likely have stayed forever.

- The address book she uses that day contains the number of times the family moved since their arrival in America. *"One hand, five homes, a lifetime in a fist."* (p.167)

Cross Culture

- Aside from the occasional return trip to India to visit or mourn family, the Gangulis spend eight months in Calcutta on an extended sabbatical leave. Gogol and Sonia are now the essential immigrants, the outsiders. The pot has melted, and although they are somewhat familiar with Bengali customs and activities, they prefer the American way.

- Their eight months in India is summed up in eight pages in the novel – a significant achievement in writing. (see Writing Style, p.41) When they arrive, the children are surrounded by people they do not feel close to, and they watch their familiar but stodgy parents transform themselves into confident, warmer, more relaxed strangers. But it is Sonia and Gogol who are out of their element.

> *They stand out in their bright, expensive sneakers, American haircuts, backpacks slung over one shoulder. Once inside, he and Sonia are given cups of Horlick's, plates of syrupy, spongy rossogollas for which they have no appetite but which they dutifully eat. They have their feet traced onto pieces of paper, and a servent is sent to Bata to bring back rubber slippers for them to wear indoors.* (p.82)

> *Of all the people who surround them at practically all times, Sonia is his only ally, the only person to speak and sit and see as he does.* (p.84)

- At the end of the few pages that describe their journey, the family returns to their American life. The first thing they notice is *"the space, ... the uncompromising silence that surrounds them."* (p.87) The next thing the kids do is call up their friends, *"who are happy enough to see them but ask them nothing about where they've been ... the eight months are put behind them, quickly shed, quickly forgotten, like clothes worn for a special occasion, or for a season that has passed."* (p.88)

- But the trip has had an effect. Gogol's visit to the Taj Mahal inspires him to become an architect, a field into which he merges the artistic talent that came to him from his maternal grandfather with his own.

Assimilation *cultural identity, belonging, loyalty*

- The novel makes it clear that Lahiri's sympathies lie not only with new immigrants, but with their children as well. She states that her novel is about assimilation as an imperfect process. It is doubly hard on the kids who must assimilate twice – first to their peer group whose names, language, and customs are different from those in the home that they are growing up in, and a second time to their parents' cultural group, whose names, language, and customs are different from what they see around them.

  Is there such a thing as a perfect assimilation?

- Immigrants experience split-level life – not only by physically living away from their original families, but also through the cultural differences between themselves and their children. The real immigrants, the parents, at least have the comfort of their expatriate community as support. But we see that Gogol and Moushumi, the next generation, feel discomfort both inside and outside their homes.

- Ashima does her best to ease the transition into her new life. First, she sets up a circle of friends, whose only common ground is that they all come from Calcutta. They celebrate familiar holidays and festivals and cheer each other on in the milestone events of their children, such as *annaprasan*, the rice ceremony, which is the first official rite in a child's life. (p.38) Every year following, Ashima will make a special rice pudding for each of her children's birthdays, and she will serve it beside a piece of American birthday cake.

- Food continues to level the cultural playing field, and Ashima concedes to her children's enthusiasm for American-style food and celebrations.

  > *They learn to roast turkeys, albeit rubbed with garlic and cumin and cayenne, at Thanksgiving, to nail a wreath to their door in December, to wrap woolen scarves around snowmen, to color boiled eggs violet*

*and pink at Easter and hide them around the house.
For the sake of Gogol and Sonia they celebrate, with
progressively increasing fanfare, the birth of Christ, an
event the children look forward to far more than the
worship of Durga and Saraswati ... [a tradition that]
can't compare to Christmas, when they hang stockings
on the fireplace mantel, and set out cookies and milk
for Santa Claus, and receive heaps of presents, and stay
home from school.* (p.64, 65)

- Ashima even makes the children an "American" dinner each week,
  sometimes Shake 'n Bake chicken, other times Hamburger Helper.
  For lunches, she makes bologna or roast beef sandwiches, so that
  Gogol will not stand out in the lunchroom. In this way, Ashima creates a double load for herself by preparing the food of two cultures
  simultaneously. For example, she could have fed the entire country
  on the menu she devised for Gogol's fourteenth birthday. *"All this is
  less stressful to her than the task of feeding a handful of American
  children, half of whom always claim they are allergic to milk, all of
  whom refuse to eat the crusts of their bread."* (p.72)

- While Ashima has little difficulty marrying the two cultures in her
  life, Gogol is very conflicted. His conflict takes the form of rebellion.
  He is attracted to women from outside his community, like Ruth and
  Maxine. He even marries Moushumi, not so much out of love, as
  out of a perverse form of rebellion. (see Marriage, p.56)

- Gogol resents the pressure to maintain old-world traditions and
  expectations, which are largely unfamiliar and uncomfortable. He
  experiences two clashes – generational and cultural. The ways of
  American life are a mystery to Gogol's parents, while the ways of
  Indian life are mysterious to him. Part of his solution is to distance
  himself by moving to New York, *"a place which his parents do not
  know well."* (p.126) Ashima is confused. *"Having been deprived of
  the company of her own parents upon moving to America, her children's independence, their need to keep their distance from her, is
  something she will never understand."* (p.166)

- When Maxine asks Gogol if his parents expect him to bring home an Indian girl as a bride, *"he feels angry at his parents then, wishing they could be otherwise, knowing in his heart what the answer is. 'I don't know … I guess so. It doesn't matter what they want.'"* (p.139) But eventually, Gogol discovers that it does matter to him, very much. What Gogol eventually learns is that he can't escape his family or his background; both follow him everywhere, haunting him like Gogol of "The Overcoat."

- Gogol's assimilation and re-integration into his family and culture come after the loss of his father. (see Alienation, Loss, p.31) After identifying his father's body, Gogol enters Ashoke's Cleveland apartment, preferring to stay there overnight as opposed to renting an anonymous hotel room. It is here that Gogol begins the long journey of reconnection. For the first time, he understands *"the guilt that his parents carried inside, at being able to do nothing when their parents had died in India, of arriving weeks, sometimes months later, when there was nothing left to do."* (p.179)

- Gogol then does the only thing he can. He remembers seeing his father's sorrow at his own father's death. Although it meant nothing to him at the time, Gogol is now comforted by being able to express his grief in a concrete way: *"it [is] a Bengali son's duty to shave his head in the wake of a parent's death."* (p.179) And that is just what he does. He has found an opening in the path of belonging. His rejection of Maxine and his later marriage to Moushumi are just stops on the journey.

WRITING STYLE

WRITING STYLE

General Elements

- The strength and beauty of Lahiri's prose is not immediately evident, because it is quiet, unassuming, and undramatic. Because she is primarily a writer of short stories, she brings these skills to her novel. The novel is again a backhanded reference to the novel's namesake, the short story "The Overcoat." (see Keys to the Novel, p.7)

- There is an emotional remove and distance behind the controlled and careful word choices, a *"melancholy poise"* that Lahiri uses for the tone in this novel, which comes from her reading of Russian novels. Like the Russian writers who come before her, Lahiri uses the smallest of details to give much information. For example, when Gogol is fourteen, he and his family go to India on one of his father's sabbaticals. There is one page of description for each of the eight months they spend there. (see Cross Culture, p.34) The entire trip is described in highly general and superficial terms. There is no sudden birth or rebirth of love for India.

So few pages, so few details, so many emotional facts.

Narration

- The narration of the novel feels as though it is coming through a filter – the characters feel distant until Lahiri suddenly drops down and zeroes in on a significant thought. Then the narration has a living, breathing quality that immediately draws the reader back into the story. (see Photographs, p.57)

- The entire novel is written in the present tense, which further gives us the impression that we are dropping in on the ongoing lives of the characters. This technique reinforces the idea of the narrator as an outside observer.

- In turn, this parallels Gogol's sense of being an outsider, in the same way his namesake is an outsider in the Russian short story, and in the same way Gogol, the writer, was an outsider to his peers.

Juxtaposition

- Juxtaposition is another literary tool that Lahiri uses throughout the novel. She starts by juxtaposing the real and the fictional Gogol, pointing out that superficial features of immigration can overtake the reader like an overcoat and can simply cover up the real information that lies beneath stereotypes and misinformation.

- The Russian Gogol used juxtaposition and the detailed descriptions of seemingly trivial situations to clarify what matters and what does not. In his writing, he filtered out all the unnecessary information, and Lahiri does the same.

- The real Gogol presented absurd scenarios partly because that was his nature. He was unable to separate himself from the world of his characters and their situations. The fictional Gogol is unable to merge with his family's cultural character and perspective. Lahiri juxtaposes the real and the fictional to strengthen the effect of each.

- How each Gogol gets his name is an absurd corollary to a very real and important process. Each Gogol, especially the one in this novel, must find a presentable identity that will distinctly fit the many parts that make up his persona. Our Gogol tries everything, both outside and inside his community, and nothing seems to work.

Alliteration

- Lahiri makes a powerful point of connection with the technique of alliteration, the pairing of words beginning with the same letter. She begins with Gogol's name – Gogol Ganguli – modeled after the name of his namesake – Akaky Akakievich. (see Nikolai Gogol and The Overcoat, p.14)

- Next are Gogol's parents, whose names both begin with the letter A (Ashima and Ashoke). They fit together beautifully, having grown into love easily in America (which also starts with an A).

- The technique gets very interesting when we come to Gogol's important relationships with Maxine and Moushumi. Both of their names start with the same letter, and they fit together because they represent the balanced extremes of Gogol's conflict with culture. There is no common ground for him in either relationship. (see Moushumi, p.21; Maxine, p.18)

Pathetic Fallacy

- Lahiri is not above using the traditional literary technique of pathetic fallacy. She matches the weather outside to the emotional climate inside the character. And she does it beautifully.

- On the day that Ashoke dies, Lahiri describes the sun's strength at three o'clock in the afternoon as *"already draining from the sky. It is the sort of day that seems to end minutes after it begins, defeating Ashima's intentions to spend it fruitfully, the inevitability of nightfall distracting her … It's one of the things she's always hated about life here: these chilly, abbreviated days of early winter, darkness descending mere hours after noon."* (p.163)

- In these few words and sentences, we are told of a life that will be ending all too quickly (Ashoke's), and another life (Ashima's) that is different from what she had originally imagined. We also see that she has not disliked all of it, only some parts.

- Even though the narration feels sparse, the observations come out of our own experiences and so they feel familiar. As readers, we fill in the details. (see Dostoyevsky, p.45)

Literary Allusions

- Lahiri's connection to Nikolai Gogol and his story, "The Overcoat," is dealt with extensively in other sections of this guide. However, there are a couple of other allusions that are important to the overview of this wonderful novel.

Dostoyevsky

- Dostoyevsky once said, *"We all came out of Gogol's overcoat."* Aside from the obvious allusion to Nikolai Gogol's work, this sentence has become part of the world's lexicon and refers to many different things. Dostoyevsky directed the comment to other writers, with Gogol as the head of the pack. In that sense, this novel comes directly out of Gogol's overcoat.

- In connection to her story and characters, Lahiri uses Dostoyevsky's quote to refer to the overcoat of common ideas, values, and traditions that we inherit from our families or from a specific cultural background and that change us as we grow. There is also an overcoat of universal feelings and common experiences that everyone can relate to just as human beings.

Virginia Woolf

- Lahiri creates a brilliant literary analogy for the sense of distance in the scene that describes the family's trip to the ocean. When they reach the water's edge, Gogol and his father walk out to the end of the breakwater, where there is a small lighthouse. The trip is intended to address the physical barrier (between India and America) created by the ocean. (see Cultural Divide, p.33; see Ocean, p.59)

- In a tribute to Virginia Woolf's **To The Lighthouse**, Lahiri alludes to the outing as a day trip, but it represents everyone's life passage, which is filled with individual and unique experiences. These experiences help to build the person each of us is to become. However, like the efforts of the Ramsay family to reach the lighthouse in Woolf's story, it is not the destination that is important, but the journey.

- In a similar way, Gogol has not completed the journey toward his final identity, but we see that he is well on his way.

WRITING STRUCTURE

Setting

Photography

Writing Structure

- The short story structure of this novel has been discussed in other sections. **The Namesake** is a full-length novel that extensively uses the characteristics of short story writing (see Keys, p.7), but here Lahiri has added more characters, more action and interaction, and a deeper exploration of the themes. The elements of the short story allow Lahiri to present her themes vividly and without extraneous embellishment. Despite the brevity of this novel, it does not lack for rich detail or complex emotional involvement. Each word is carefully selected and each word counts. This is an extraordinary accomplishment.

Setting

- Notwithstanding that the novel is set primarily in the United States, there is a sense of dual setting that comes out of the intentional interlocking of India and America in a cultural conflict felt by the characters. It is this conflict that becomes the fictional landscape of the novel.

- Whether the scene is set in Boston or New York, images of Calcutta hover in the background (and vice versa) on the family's journey across the ocean. There is a constant sense of struggle suspended over the characters about what it means to live and be raised in America and about how to cope with having left India.

- Each part of the setting overlaps and influences the other. This is Gogol's ever-present challenge – to find a way to merge the two successfully.

Photography   *time lapse*

- At times, the narrative of the novel feels as though it is coming through a filtered camera lens. There are close-ups and long shots. The result is a kind of time-lapse verbal photography, in which Lahiri races through some details while she lets others unfold in a slowly relaxed and significant way. It is the combination of fast and slow that allows these tiny details, facts, words, and images to compose and to sharpen the whole picture. In other words, she creates vivid scenes and images that become fixed in the reader's mind.

- It is for this reason that Mira Nair's film is so successful. Lahiri made Nair's job easy by putting the cinematic elements in place in the novel. Only the actors were missing until Nair set them on location. (see Film, p.67)

SYMBOLS

Identity (Name, Overcoat)

Culture (Food, Marriage)

Journey (Photographs,

Ocean, Train)

SYMBOLS

The symbols of this novel will be grouped according to theme rather than as individual items of representation.

Symbols of Identity   *name, overcoat*

Name

- Names can be equated with labels and other words that identify a person or item. Therefore, as a symbol, a name is an excellent icon to portray uniqueness and distinctiveness.

- Both Gogol and Moushumi are unhappy with their names, and this unhappiness spills over into their separate lives and their life together. While visiting their friends, Astrid and Donald, they discuss the choice of possible names for their baby. The discussion is animated, and many name books are consulted. Immediately, Gogol and Moushumi become outsiders to the conversation, because their names are not listed in any of these reference books.

- It is in this scene that Moushumi humiliates Gogol when she reveals that he wasn't named Nikhil at birth. He would prefer to keep this fact a secret because, even so long after his father's death, he still feels guilty about changing his name. Gogol tells the group that people should not be named until they turn eighteen and can name themselves. He feels that there is no perfect name for anyone.
What is your feeling about Gogol's opinion? When is the optimal moment to name a child? Who should choose and bestow the name?

Overcoat

- In the section on Lahiri's life (see Author Information, p.8), we saw that her father was a librarian and her mother a schoolteacher. These small details are reflected in the novel, but in mirror image – Gogol's father is the teacher, and his mother works in the library. The idea of a reflective image is interesting, because a mirror projects how we look to ourselves and to others. Usually in literature, the mirror exists as a symbol of identity. But Lahiri has chosen a different symbol for this theme – an overcoat, taken from Gogol's short story of the same name.

- The overcoat has been extensively dealt with in other sections, but it bears another look here because it is the overriding symbol of the novel. Identity is everyone's overcoat. It must integrate all the individual characteristics that we are born with – familial, cultural, geographic, historical, and those of our own unique genetic personality. All of these things are summed up in every person's name. The name must fit well if it is to be a protective and distinguishing mantle. (see Suggested Beginnings, p.68)

Symbols of Culture *food, marriage*

Food

- Food marks special events in every culture but has even more significance for immigrants. Food becomes their link to each other and to the traditions from home. Their traditional food and the manner of its preparation is the one thing they are able to bring with them across the ocean.

- Ashima tries to use food as a leveler of cultural differences. (see Assimilation, p.36) Lahiri describes Ashima's loving preparation of food in delightful detail, because it is through food that Ashima truly identifies herself from the beginning of the novel to the end.

- The descriptions start with the rice ceremonies for both Gogol and Sonia. Called *annaprasan*, this ritual marks the baby's first feeding of solid food and takes place when the child is about seven or eight months old – old enough to reach out and grasp what is offered. The baby is offered a plate holding three things: a sample of soil, a pen, and money, representing the possibility of becoming a landowner, scholar, or businessperson. Gogol is confused and touches nothing. Crying, he already begins his pull away from tradition. (p.40) Sonia, on the other hand, is the true American – she tries to take it all! (p.63)

- The food experience culminates in Ashima's last party on Pemberton Road. She is about to sell the house and live half-time in each of her homes – India and the United States. While she is preparing her feast, her memories pop up just like the croquettes she is frying in oil. She remembers the good times and the bad; she reflects on how independent she has grown, both with and without her husband; and she reflects on the differences in her own marriage and those of her children's. Most importantly, she has grown comfortable with who she has become and who her children are. She has successfully bridged the gap across the ocean.

How do the other characters fare?

Marriage

- Normally, in a literary analysis, marriage would be listed under themes, but in the context of this novel, the concept of marriage should be considered a symbol of culture and a symbol of the ultimate integration and connection between two people. Lahiri is not discussing the pros and cons of the married state but is looking at the perspective and impact of marriage in the two separate cultures.

- Ashima and Ashoke meet only once before their marriage. The pair rely on the time-honored tradition of a marriage arranged by their parents. The couple only have to seal the deal by agreeing, which they do. (see Ashima and Ashoke, p.17) On the other hand, Gogol and Moushumi marry in spite of their parents' endorsement. Both of their mothers had wanted them to meet and finally they do. Surprisingly, they like each other and feel comfortable together. But they mistake comfort and familiarity for love, and in the end, the marriage fails. Where their parents had assumed nothing but hoped to simply get along and successfully raise a family together, Gogol and Moushumi entertained much higher hopes for their marriages; influenced by the western culture in which they were raised, they hoped for and expected a love match. It's curious then, that they married each other, since neither of them was, in fact, marrying for love. While on the face of it, both Gogol and Moushumi are marrying to please their parents, their marriage seems to be a perverse form of rebellion against their culture. (see Assimilation, p.36)

  Sometimes [Moushumi] wondered if it was her horror of being married to someone she didn't love that had caused her, subconsciously, to shut herself off. (p.214)

- However, culture demands attention no matter how hard we try to throw off its overcoat. Moushumi cancels her wedding to Graham, because he cannot connect with her family. It is *"one thing for her to reject her background, to be critical of her family's heritage, another to hear it from him."* (p.217)

- It is mostly on the rebound that she becomes involved with Gogol. Their wedding is *"an hour-long watered-down Hindu ceremony on a platform covered with sheets. ... Nothing has been rehearsed or explained to them beforehand."* (p.222) They are quite removed from the traditions of marriage that now surround them, but the fact of the matter is that they marry with the relieved blessings of their families.

- Sadly, as much as Ashima had always hoped that Gogol would wear his cultural traditions easily, she accepts his divorce from Moushumi. Ashima has moved beyond cultural expectations. She is happy that *"they have not considered it their duty to stay married, as the Bengalis of Ashoke and Ashima's generation do. They are not willing to accept, to adjust, to settle for something less than their ideal of happiness. That pressure has given way, in the case of the subsequent generation, to American common sense."* (p.276)

   What impacts a marriage more – love or tradition? Should there be a balance between the two, or should one concept outweigh the other?

Symbols of Journey

photographs (memory), ocean, train

Photographs

- It is easy to overlook the number of photographs taken and present in the novel, because a picture is something we all take for granted; it is a familiar constant in our lives. Yet photographs importantly record our lives moment by moment. Photographs provide the memories that chronicle the journeys that our lives take.

- The camera is present at Gogol's birth and, with Ashoke's later purchase of an instamatic camera, continues to archive events:

  A first photograph, somewhat overexposed, is taken by Dr. Gupta ... [Ashima] stands squinting into the sun. Her husband looks on from one side ... smiling with his head lowered. "Gogol enters the world," his father will eventually write on the back in Bengali letters. (p.29)

- Photographs are taken at all the special ceremonies and occasions in the children's lives, including the *annaprasan* (rice ceremony). Each time they move, Ashoke takes pictures of all the rooms in the house. The family poses for pictures on each family trip. The only time the camera is not present is when it is forgotten on the outing to the ocean. Without the camera, Ashoke tells Gogol he will have to simply remember the moment. Lahiri presents memory as the mind's camera.

  "Try to remember it always," he said ... "Remember that you and I made this journey, that we went together to a place where there was nowhere left to go." (p.187)

- Aside from trips as a family, Gogol and his father rarely did anything together. They hardly even spoke about the important things between them. Such was the divide between them; it was not lack of love, but simply a lack of things in common.

- But Ashoke had planted a strong seed of memory for Gogol, one that has duly recorded important connections between them. Its marker is the single photograph that was used at Ashoke's funeral. *"It is the photograph more than anything that draws Gogol back to the house again and again, and one day, stepping out of the bathroom on his way to bed and glancing at his father's smiling face, he realizes that this is the closest thing his father has to a grave."* (p.189) Although Ashoke dies part way through the story, his influence affects Gogol more after his death than while he was alive. (Gogol and The Overcoat, p.14)

Ocean

- The ocean lies physically between America and India and is a wonderful symbol for other gaps and divides – geographic, cultural, generational, and emotional.

    o The grandmother's letter containing Gogol's name is lost somewhere over the ocean. The family flies back and forth across the ocean between the United States and India. Most of the family's American road trips are to the edge of the ocean.

    o There are oceans of mutual misunderstanding and emotional distance in each of Gogol's relationships – with Ruth, Maxine, and even with Moushumi.

    o Gogol and his father are constantly approaching each other from different sides of the ocean. Ashoke desperately wants Gogol to understand his experiences in India and how they affected him. But Gogol will not take the time to listen until it is almost too late.

- When Gogol does finally hear the details of Ashoke's accident and how that incident led to his name, he asks his father whether he views him through a lens of pain and suffering. Ashoke denies this and says he looks at Gogol as an image of the future. In his mind's eye, Gogol is the photographic evidence of what has become a beautiful new life with a wonderful family. (see Photographs, p.57)

- The Ganguli family journey has not been just an ordinary outing. It has physically taken them across the ocean and has culturally taken them even further. Each member of the family has journeyed along the metaphorical continuum of life to establish a new identity.

Train

The overriding symbol of the novel is that of the journey of life, not as a straight excursion but one that continuously shuffles back and forth as a result of the changes and adjustments that need to be made at every turn. With the exception of the plane rides across the ocean, the primary mode of transportation in the novel is the train.

- Both Gogol and his father have significant experiences on the train. On Ashoke's fateful train ride he meets Ghosh, a Bengali who has returned from abroad, who tells him to leave India and follow his dreams. Ashoke goes to America.

- Gogol travels back and forth from home and school by train. These trips take him out of his Bengali community in a literal and metaphorical way. It is on the train that he meets Ruth, the first of his non-Indian relationships. The cultural clash is so strong for him that he cannot bear the thought of bringing Ruth home. His two worlds cannot merge.

- When he later meets Maxine, he is no longer Gogol but has renamed himself Nikhil. This allows him to bring Max into the house, but only once.

- One day on a trip home, the train is delayed because someone had committed suicide by jumping in front of it. Now we have a scene from another literary allusion, Tolstoy's **Anna Karenina**, which fore-shadows Ashoke's death. The train's delay has made Ashoke very nervous and has brought back all his terrible memories. He finally tells Gogol the whole story behind his name. For the first time, Gogol is mature enough to listen.

> *"He listens, stunned ... For an instant his father is a stranger, a man who has kept a secret, has survived a tragedy, a man whose past he does not fully know."*
> (p.123)

- As the train continues to shuttle from city to city, Gogol goes from relationship to relationship. He can't successfully decide on a final destination, because he is always distracted by the stops along the way. On his previous train rides, Gogol always has a seatmate. It is only on his final train ride home, after his father's death, that Gogol is finally alone on the train. There is no one sitting beside him – except himself.

- And this is the moment when he begins to reflect – on his home, on his parents' lives and their mutual love, on their separation from those they love, on his own self-imposed isolation, on the fact that he can no longer see his own origins.

- It is only now, when he is utterly alone, that he realizes that his name truly does have a meaning and a fit. It is only now when he is completely by himself that he finally hears *"the sound of his pet name uttered by his father as he has been accustomed to hearing it all his life."* (p.124) His name is no longer a symbol of shame, but a symbol of courage, as represented by his parents, who left behind everything and everyone they loved in order to create new hope in a new life.

- Gogol knows that he does not have such courage – yet. But he is finally aware that he has a namesake with a connection that is uniquely his – it is his identity and no one else's – there is no other Nikhil Gogol Ganguli. His final step is to slip on the overcoat of this identity, an act that comforts him, and he goes home.

- The journey of Gogol's life had started with a train wreck.

  > *In so many ways, his family's life feels like a string of accidents, unforeseen, unintended, one incident begetting another ... There was the disappearance of the name Gogol's great-grandmother had chosen for him ... This had led, in turn, to the accident of his being named Gogol, defining and distressing him for so many years. He had tried to correct that randomness, that*

error. And yet it had not been possible to reinvent himself fully, to break from that mismatched name. His marriage had been something of a misstep as well. And the way his father had slipped away from them, that had been the worst accident of all ... And yet these events have formed Gogol, shaped him, determined who he is. They were things for which it was impossible to prepare but which one spent a lifetime looking back at, trying to accept, interpret, comprehend. Things that should never have happened, that seemed out of place and wrong, these were what prevailed, what endured, in the end. (p.287)

- Gogol's journey is not yet over, but it is back on track.

LAST THOUGHTS

Conclusion

The Film

Suggested Beginnings

LAST THOUGHTS

Conclusion

- Gogol's life has been shaped and reshaped not only by his name but also by Ashoke's life and death. When Ashoke gives Gogol a copy of the book of short stories by his namesake, he inscribes it as follows: *"The man who gave you his name, from the man who gave you your name."* (p.288)

- The name "Gogol" is one that Gogol spent his lifetime hating, but it was the first and most important thing his parents gave him. Lahiri asks the question: How do we integrate all the different parts of where we come from with who we are? How do we filter out the cultural treasures from the trash? How do we become comfortable with who we are today?

- The novel ends full circle – Gogol is born and then reborn, just like his father after the train accident. Both are given second chances. And in the final scene, Gogol sits down to read the second most important thing his parents gave him – the book written by the author for whom he is named.

> *The givers and the keepers of Gogol's name are far from him now. One dead. Another, a widow, on the verge of a different sort of departure ... Without people in the world to call him Gogol, no matter how long he himself lives, Gogol Ganguli will, once and for all, vanish from the lips of loved ones, and so, cease to exist. Yet the thought of this eventual demise provides no sense of victory, no solace. It provides no solace at all.* (p.289)

- At this point, Gogol is alone and divorced from Moushumi. His sister, Sonia, has a new husband, who is not Bengali, and the world, even in Ashima's terms, has softened and blurred. Gogol is about to start a new job in a company that will publicly use his name in its formal identity.

- As our story closes, Gogol is finally on the right track. But now Gogol himself is asking questions. Will he successfully assimilate all the separate parts of his identity? Will he become comfortable with both? Who will he eventually become?

- Lahiri leaves the answers open and invites us to talk about them at the same moment that Gogol starts to read the book. We know this because in the last words in the novel Lahiri switches from the present to the future tense.

> *As the hours of the evening pass he will grow distracted, anxious to return to his room, to be alone, to read the book he had once forsaken, has abandoned until now. Until moments ago it was destined to disappear*

from his life altogether, but he has salvaged it by chance, as his father was pulled from a crushed train forty years ago. He leans back against the headboard, adjusting a pillow behind his back. In a few minutes he will go downstairs, join the party, his family … For now, he starts to read.

The Film   *by Mira Nair*

- *The Namesake* is in the theaters and it is a very good film. It is directed by Mira Nair (**Monsoon Wedding, Mississipi Masala**) and Kal Penn plays Gogol. The actors who play Ashoke and Ashima are also both excellent. Jhumpa Lahiri makes a cameo appearance in the scene depicting the *annaprasan* ceremony. (see the Bookclub-in-a-Box website for the discussion guide to the film of *The Namesake*.)

- This film is Mira Nair's most personal project to date. The critics are mixed in their reviews, but we highly recommend it. The film is true to the book and presents the people and events exactly as Lahiri describes. Mira Nair made this film as a likeness, a namesake, of the novel – not necessarily as a film with its own story. Having said that, the film does stand on its own.

- It all came to be when Nair happened to be reading **The Namesake** while she was grieving for her Ugandan-born mother-in-law, who lived and then died in America. Nair was devastated by the thought that this woman, who had once known the rich earth and sunshine of Uganda, would forever be covered by New Jersey's wintery elements.

- Inspired by this personal incident and more, Nair decided to make the film. Here is how she explains what it all means to her:

[Lahiri's novel] encompasses in a deep humane way the tale of millions of us who have left one home for another, who have known what it means to combine the old ways with the new world, who have left the shadow of our parents to find ourselves for the first time. (Murray)

- This novel too is about more than just the immigrant experience and its aftermath; it is also about coming of age, about growing up and into an identity that we are handed at birth. And it is about all the other things that have been discussed so far.

Suggested Beginnings

1. This book is centered on the naming of a baby, which is an important and time-honored tradition in every culture, but sometimes the process and the reasons for the choice are absurdly irrelevant.

What are your thoughts about your own names – are you comfortable with your name or names? What are your thoughts about Gogol's name?

2. The Namesake is a book about names and naming, about identity, and what influences that identity. Lahiri had once actually known someone named Gogol, and she wanted to write a book about a boy whose peculiar name haunted him and weighed him down. She felt it was the perfect metaphor for the experience of growing up as the child of immigrants, so she uses the novel to explore that issue as well.

Do we grow into our names? What are the effects of the cultural heirlooms we inherit from our parents? Is there a clash of cultural ideas, values, behavior? How do manage that clash?

3. Lahiri uses the device of the journey to show how Gogol and others like him try to cross the gulf between two cultures. He travels with his family to India, but he doesn't feel any emotional attachment to that country. He travels with his family to the ocean, symbolic of the division between the cultures, but his emotions don't align with his father's.

Is it possible to successfully integrate heritage and culture? Is this equally true for both parents and children? Does cultural inheritance weigh down or change identity and the relationship with others? Can Gogol ever escape how he presents himself? Is he haunted by the confusion of his cultural identities in the same way as Gogol's Akaky haunts those who had challenged and made fun of his identity?

4. Modern custom accepts name and cultural hybrids as a way of integrating two identities (parental, ethnic). For example, children are given a new hyphenated name made up of the surnames of the parents. Ethnic and political identities are merged in such terms as Asian-American or American-Italian.

Consider these practices in your discussion of this novel.

5. Gogol advocates allowing a child to choose his or her own name at the age of eighteen.

Is there an optimal time for a child to do this? Should a child select his or her name? What should the child be called in the meantime? What effect would all of this have on the child's sense of identity?

FROM THE NOVEL

Quotes

From the Novel ...

Memorable quotes from the text of
The Namesake

PAGE 1. On a sticky August evening two weeks before her due date, Ashima Ganguli stands in the kitchen ... combining Rice Krispies and Planters peanuts and chopped red onion in a bowl. She adds salt, lemon juice, thin slices of green chili pepper, wishing there were mustard oil to pour into the mix. Ashima has been consuming this concoction throughout her pregnancy, a humble approximation of the snack sold for pennies on Calcutta sidewalks and on railway platforms throughout India, spilling from newspaper cones.

PAGE 3. It is the first time in her life she has slept alone, surrounded by strangers; all her life she has slept either in a room with her parents, or with Ashoke at her side. She wishes the curtains were open, so that she could talk to the American women.

PAGE 7. She was nineteen, in the middle of her studies, in no rush to be a bride. And so, obediently but without expectation, she had untangled and rebraided her hair, wiped away the kohl that had smudged below her eyes ... The sheer parrot green sari she pleated and tucked into her petticoat had been laid out for her on the bed by her mother.

PAGE 14. Ashoke was always devastated when Akaky was robbed in "a square that looked to him like a dreadful desert," leaving him cold and vulnerable, and Akaky's death, some pages later, never failed to bring tears to his eyes. In some ways the story made less sense each time he read it, the scenes he pictured so vividly, and absorbed so fully, growing more elusive and profound. Just as Akaky's ghost haunted the final pages, so did it haunt a place deep in Ashoke's soul, shedding light on all that was irrational, all that was inevitable about the world.

PAGE 21. It is not the memory of the pain that haunts him. ... It is the memory of waiting before he was rescued, and the persistent fear, rising up in his throat, that he might not have been rescued at all ... He was born twice in India, and then a third time, in America. Three lives by thirty ... For this he thanks his parents, and their parents, and the parents of their parents ... Instead of thanking God he thanks Gogol, the Russian writer who had saved his life.

PAGE 25. An infant doesn't really need a name. He needs to be fed and blessed, to be given some gold and silver, to be patted on the back after feedings and held carefully behind the neck. Names can wait. In India parents take their time. It wasn't unusual for years to pass before the right name, the best possible name, was determined.

PAGE 48. The Gangulis have moved to a university town outside Boston. As far as they know, they are the only Bengali residents ... He shares, along with the other members of his department, the services of an elderly secretary named Mrs. Jones [who] is about his own mother's age.

Mrs. Jones leads a life that Ashoke's mother would consider humiliating: eating alone, driving herself to work in snow and sleet, seeing her children and grandchildren, at most, three or four times a year.

PAGE 51. There are pictures of Gogol opening up the refrigerator, pretending to talk on the phone. He is a sturdily built child, with full cheeks but already pensive features. When he poses for the camera he has to be coaxed into a smile.

PAGE 55. "Finish," his father says, glancing up from his magazine. "Don't play with food that way."

"I'm full, Baba."

"There's still some food on your plate."

His father's plate is polished clean, the chicken bones denuded of cartilage and chewed to a pinkish pulp, the bay leaf and cinnamon stick as good as new. Ashoke shakes his head at Gogol, disapproving, unyielding. Each day Ashoke is pained by the half-eaten sandwiches people toss into garbage cans on campus, apples abandoned after one or two bites. "Finish it, Gogol. At your age I ate tin."

PAGE 60. At the end of his first day he is sent home with a letter to his parents from Mrs. Lapidus, folded and stapled to a string around his neck, explaining that due to their son's preference he will be known as Gogol at school. What about the parents' preference? Ashima and Ashoke wonder, shaking their heads. But since neither of them feels comfortable pressing the issue, they have no choice but to give in.

PAGE 65. When Gogol is in the third grade, they send him to Bengali language and culture lessons every other Saturday, held in the home of one of their friends. For when Ashima and Ashoke close their eyes it never fails to unsettle them, that their children sound just like Americans, expertly conversing in a language that still at times confounds them, in accents they are accustomed not to trust.

PAGE 76. From the little he knows about Russian writers, it dismays him that his parents chose the weirdest namesake. Leo or Anton, he could have lived with. Alexander, shortened to Alex, he would have greatly preferred. But Gogol sounds ludicrous to his ears, lacking dignity or gravity.

What dismays him most is the irrelevance of it all. Gogol, he's been tempt- ed to tell his father on more than one occasion, was his father's favorite author, not his. Then again, it's his own fault. He could have been known, at school at least, as Nikhil. That one day, that first day of kindergarten, which he no longer remembers, could have changed everything. He could have been Gogol only fifty percent of the time.

PAGE 89. Mr. Lawson distributes ... copies of an anthology, *Short Story Classics* ... Gogol's copy is particularly battered ... He looks at the table of contents, sees Gogol listed after Faulkner, before Hemingway. The sight of it printed in capital letters on the crinkly page upsets him viscerally. It's as though the name were a particularly unflattering snapshot of himself that makes him want to say in his defense, "That's not really me."

PAGE 104, 105. At the last minute he registers for a drawing class in the evenings. He doesn't tell his parents about the drawing class, something they would consider frivolous at this stage of his life, in spite of the fact that his own grandfather was an artist. They were already distressed that he hasn't settled on a major and a profession ... his parents expect him to be, if not an engineer, then a doctor, a lawyer, an economist at the very least. These were the fields that brought them to America ... the professions that have earned them security and respect.

PAGE 107. [Sonia] is in high school now ... going to the dances Gogol never went to himself, already going to parties at which both boys and girls are present. Her braces have come off her teeth, revealing a confident, fre- quent, American smile. ... Ashima lives in fear that Sonia will color a streak of [her hair] blond, as Sonia has threatened on more than one occasion to do, and that she will have additional holes pierced in her earlobes at the mall.

PAGE 132 [Maxine] tells him this is the house she's grown up in, mention- ing casually that she'd moved back six months ago after living with a man in Boston, an arrangement that had not worked out. When he asks if she plans to look for a place of her own she says ... "I love this house. There's really nowhere else I'd rather live." For all her sophistication he finds the fact that she's moved back with her parents ... endearingly old-fashioned; it is something he cannot picture himself doing at this stage in his life.

PAGE 139. And so he moves in with her in a way, bringing a few bags of clothes, nothing else. His futon and his table, his kettle and toaster and television and the rest of his things, remain on Amsterdam Avenue. His answering machine continues to record his messages. He continues to receive his mail there, in a nameless metal box.

PAGE 148. [Gogol is] irritated by his parents' perpetual fear of disaster. When he returns to the house, the lunch is set out, too rich for the weather. Along with the samosas, there are breaded chicken cutlets, chickpeas with tamarind sauce, lamb biryani, chutney made with tomatoes from the garden. It is a meal he knows it has taken his mother over a day to prepare, and yet the amount of effort embarrasses him. The water glasses are already filled, plates and forks and paper napkins set on the dining room table they use only for special occasions, with uncomfortable high-backed chairs and seats upholstered in gold velvet.

PAGE 162. Three afternoons a week and two Saturdays a month, she works at the public library ... It is Ashima's first job in America, the first since before she was married. She signs her small paychecks over to Ashoke, and he deposits them for her at the bank into their account ... She is friendly with the other women who work at the library, most of them also with grown children ... They are the first American friends she has made in her life.

PAGE 168. "I'm very sorry, ma'am," the young woman repeats. "We've been trying to reach you."

And then the young woman tells her that the patient, Ashoke Ganguli, her husband, has expired.

Expired. A word used for library cards, for magazine subscriptions. A word which, for several seconds, has no effect whatsoever on Ashima.

PAGE 180. For ten days following his father's death, he and his mother and Sonia eat a mourner's diet, forgoing meat and fish ... Gogol remembers having to do the same thing when he was younger, when his grandparents died, his mother yelling at him when he forgot one day and had a hamburger at school ... Now, sitting together at the kitchen table at six-thirty every evening, the hour feeling more like midnight through the window, his father's chair empty, this meatless meal is the only thing that seems to make sense.

PAGE 183.   Ashima has no desire to escape to Calcutta, not now.   She refuses to be so far from the place where her husband made his life, the country in which he died. "Now I know why he went to Cleveland," she tells people, refusing, even in death, to utter her husband's name. "He was teaching me how to live alone."

PAGE 191.   From time to time his mother asks him if he has a new girl-friend ... When he tells her that he isn't even thirty, she tells him that by that age she had already celebrated her tenth wedding anniversary. He is aware, without having to be told, that his father's death has accelerated certain expectations, that by now his mother wants him settled.

PAGE 210.   With both hands he pries the glasses from her face, clasping the frames where they meet her temples ... They make their way through the living room, to the bedroom ... They make love on top of the covers, quickly, efficiently, as if they've known each other's bodies for years. But when they are finished she switches on the lamp by her bed and they examine each other, quietly discovering moles and marks and ribs.

"Who would have thought," she says, her voice tired, satisfied. She is smiling, her eyes partly closed.

PAGE 227.   Only she is not Mrs. Ganguli. Moushumi has kept her last name. She doesn't adopt Ganguli, not even with a hyphen. Her own last name, Mazoomdar, is already a mouthful ... Though he hasn't admitted this to her, he'd hoped, the day they'd filled out the application for their marriage license, that she might consider otherwise ... But the thought of changing her last name to Ganguli has never crossed Moushumi's mind.

PAGE 248.   She's disappointed but not surprised. By now she's learned that his architect's mind for detail fails when it comes to everyday things. For example, he had not bothered to hide the receipt for the shawl, leaving it, along with change emptied from his pocket, on top of the bureau they share. She can't really blame him for not remembering. She herself can no longer remember the exact date of that evening. It had been a Saturday in November. But now those landmarks in their courtship have faded.

PAGE 258. "How in the world do you spell that?" [Dimitri] asked, and when she told him, he mispronounced it, as most people did ... "I'll just call you Mouse."

The nickname had irritated and pleased her at the same time. It made her feel foolish, but she was aware that in renaming her he had claimed her somehow, already made her his own.

PAGE 282. It had been on the train, exactly a year ago, that he'd learned of Moushumi's affair ... They were in the middle of a conversation about how to spend the coming summer, whether to rent a house in Siena with Donald and Astrid, an idea Gogol was resisting, when she'd said, "Dimitri says Siena is something out of a fairy tale." Immediately a hand had gone to her mouth, accompanied by a small intake of breath. And then, silence. "Who's Dimitri?" he'd asked. And then: "Are you having an affair?"

PAGE 287. "Gogol, the camera," his mother calls out over the crowd. "Take some pictures tonight, please? I want to remember this Christmas. Next year at this time I'll be so far away."

ACKNOWLEDGEMENTS

Acknowledgements

Apte, Sudheer. "The Namesake."
http://mostlyfiction.com/world/lahiri.htm September 7, 2003.

Beal, Daphne. "Mira Nair Interviewed". *The Believer*. Vol. 5, No.3.
McSweeney's Publishing LLC, San Francisco. April 2007.

Chatterjee, Saibal. "Mira Nair to shoot next film in Calcutta." BBC
News, December 7, 2004.

Census, 2000. "The Indian American Community in the United States of
America. http://www.outofindia.net/abroad/WashingtonDC/indian_ameri-
can_community.htm

Erlich, Victor. "Gogol." *Yale University Press*. New Haven,
Connecticut. 1969.

Lahiri, Jhumpa. "Interview with the Author."
http://hinduism.about.com/library/weekly/extra/bl-jhumpainterview.htm

Metcalfe, Stephen. "Out of the Overcoat." www.nytimes.com.
September 28, 2003.

Mudge, Alden. "Lahiri probes the immigrant identity in her first novel." Interview with the author. www.bookpage.com. September, 2003.

Murray, Rebecca. "Production Begins on 'The Namesake' Directed by Mira Nair." *About Entertainment*. March 29, 2005. www.aboutentertainment.com

Riemer, Andrew. "The Namesake." *Sydney Morning Herald*. Sydney, Australia. October 25, 2003.